PUDDING OF TRUTH

A COLLECTION OF ENGLISH LAGHUKATHAS (SHORT STORIES FLASH FICTIONS)

CHANDRESH KUMAR CHHATLANI

Dedicated to all my own,

who have supported me

in my tough time

Contents

Contents

CHAPTER ONE

Pudding of Truth

He was the greatest cook in the world; there was no dish he had not made. Even today, the whole world could experience the real sweet taste of truth, so he was going to make two special dishes of truth and lies pudding. He believed that the world would understand what is good and what is bad by eating both of these dishes.

He took two pots, put ’truth‘ in one and ’lie' in the other, poured a lot of sugar in the pot of truth, and put lot of material, which was bitter like poison, in the pot of lies. Then he put equal amount of melted butter in both the dishes and fried them completely.

He was very happy while making these dishes. He wanted a world in which everyone would realize the hidden bitterness in the lie and also be familiar with the sweetness of the truth. He tasted both the dishes after decorating in the same types of plates.

And he came to know that the truth was still bitter and the lie was sweet as usual.

CHAPTER TWO

My Memory

As usual, the old man went to the bookstore, bought all today's newspapers, and sat outside and started reading them one by one. He read each newspaper for five to six minutes, and then kept it in despair.

Seeing this, today the shopkeeper's son could not stop himself and asked him out of curiosity, "What do you see every day?"

"It's been two years... I'm looking for my photo in the newspaper..." replied the old man in a disappointed tone.

Hearing this, the shopkeeper's son laughed. He somehow stopped his laughter and asked in a sarcastic tone, "Where will your photo be printed in the newspaper?"

"Looking for the missing..." said the old man and picked up the next newspaper.

CHAPTER THREE

Triple Love

Now she was nowhere. My father used to say that what is nowhere, sometimes it is everywhere. Trying to hold the cigarette's smoke in my lungs, I started coughing as soon as I remembered this saying of my father, due to which the smoke started coming out from inside and dissolving in the air and I started thinking that the like smoke, a person dissolved in air, is nowhere.

Being a painter, I am emotional, but I lived this brutality of her, that she fell in love with two men and seeing her smile even after leaving them. She used to call her first love 'Candle Love'. He used to come after the candle was lit in the evening and stayed till the morning candle was extinguished. I was fifteen in those days. The financial condition was not good, so I sell flowers in the morning to her and other. One day while taking flowers, she asked me, "Why do these flowers of yours wither during the day and seem to be blooming at night?" I didn't have an answer. Although I could see the withering of flowers on her face countless times. Months went by, one day I saw her blowing a candle full force into her Candle Love's face. I understood that day that there are some candles which break themselves but do not melt while giving befitting reply. It was the same candle that gave birth to the painter in me. On that day my first sketch of life was made - a broken colorless candle made of white wax. Seller of colorful flowers started making colorless sketches. Talking about her, within a few days I saw that her smile is returned and she started lighting lamps instead of candles.

Her second love appears three years after the first one. By then, my profession too had reached the point of rising above from the fixed colors of the plucked flowers to unmask the unseen colors on the canvas. She even bought four of my arts. Actually, She didn't bought, whenever I made pictures of flowers, I gave that to him. In return, whatever money she gave, I took. She thoughts that it is unwise to run for marriage, however, her second love was a runner. I remember very well the day after a few years of falling in love, when she took off the gold necklace from his neck and asked me to draw a picture in which the runner could not run and could never go anywhere. But I had no such imagination. I returned necklace to her and she sobbed all the night with her head on my shoulder. The next morning, she sent me off silently but again with the same familiar smile. I really liked her sincere smile towards that runner.

After that I went to her house regularly, we used to talk but I could never tell her what I truly wish. I also afraid of her cruelty on forgetting love. I came to know last evening that she died after falling from the roof of the house and today, I am looking at her photographs while taking a puff of cigarette in her house.

I found a picture, which I had made in my imagination by wearing her a rural dress. When I was cleaning the soil on the back side of that frame, then I saw few words in her handwriting. I got curious, removed the soil and read those words, she wrote,

"Alas! Hope, if you could add color to my faded color dress! How did you become a painter? You don't even know how to paint... ME."

And when I raised my head, I saw clearly that she was standing in front of me - a colorless soilless spirit.

And the same smile floated on my lips, which was not there on her transparent lips today.

CHAPTER FOUR

Access of Pain

"Bhaiya, your elder brother is having unbearable pain in his stomach, he is asking for alcohol." A deep concern was evident in her voice when she closed the door from outside.

"Sister-in-law, how much alcohol he used to drink earlier? If he tries to quit that now, then he has to endure some pain. We have to understand that if brother drinks alcohol now, then he will probably not be able to quit this for the rest of his life." His younger brother replied.

"You're right, we won't let him drink, hey mom...you!" The daughter-in-law was surprised to see the bottle of wine in the hand of her mother-in-law standing at the door.

"Why did you procure this? And where did you get the money to purchase it?" The younger son asked his mother.

"I returned my medicine, son, couldn't bear his pain..."

CHAPTER FIVE

Surrogate Mother

"Doctor John, why did Shabana, who is admitted to your mental hospital, commit suicide?"

"Sir, her mental state was quite under control now. After becoming a surrogate mother, she was deeply shocked to be separated from the child. For ten years, she considered toys as her child. Now, for the last five years, she has been gradually getting better. These days she had even started meeting everyone.

"Then why did it happen like this, Doctor John?"

"Sir, for the first time yesterday, his surrogate son, don't know how, came to meet her, he was saying that he is scolded in the family by saying that he is born from the womb of a Muslim, and today...."

CHAPTER SIX

Powerless

There was a river of fresh water. Flowing on its way, like other rivers, it too used to join the sea. Once, a fish of that river also reached to the sea while moving along with the water. Going to the sea, she got upset. Another fish in the sea saw her, she went to him and asked, "What's wrong?"

"Yes! I'm worried about living in such salty water," fish of the river replied.

The sea fish laughed and said, "This is how water tastes."

"No, no!" The river fish replied, "Water is sweet, too."

"Water and sweet! Where?" The sea fish was amazed.

"There, that side. That's where I came from." Said the river fish pointing at the direction of the river. "Good, then let's go and see." The fish of the sea replied curiously.

"Yeah, come on. I'll be able to survive there, but can you take me there?"

"Yes sure, but why can't you swim?"

"I have been flowing along the river's current for a long time, so I am unable to swim in the opposite direction," replied the fish of the river, holding the fish of the sea.

CHAPTER SEVEN

At least try

He was running madly. The panic was clearly visible on his face. He was looking back again and again, which caused him to collide with another man. The other man asked, "Hey! Is something wrong?"

He replied in a bewildered voice, "A demon is coming to capture me." The other man looked after him, he too panicked and cried out, "Oho... He's chasing me."

The other man also started running with him. Whoever came across them would see that monster and run with them in panic. The crowd was increasing constantly. Everyone thought that the demon was coming to 0capture them. Weeks, months and even years passed away. In that crowd, many people got tired and fell, some started crawling. Some of them even stopped with courage, but seeing the terrifying face of the demon and seeing it moving towards them, they started running again.

Eventually a man, who became tired of running and his fear was turning into annoyance, turned and stood up. The demon rushed towards him, seeing that, the man also ran towards the demon with all his might and started fighting with that demon.

And within a few moments he came to know that the demon named Crisis had less power than his energy to escape him.

CHAPTER EIGHT

False Masks

After many years, the two 'friends' met each other. Both hugged each other and talked about their happiness and sorrow.

Then one asked, "How's your mask?"

The other smiled and replied, "I don't know that, but I know every color of your mask."

The first exclaimed in amazement, "Oh wow! I also understand very well every gesture of your mask, not mine."

Both started laughing by shaking hands.

At that time, they saw that a crowd was coming from afar. Seeing that, both of them put their masks on their faces.

Now both were strong opponents and enemies of each other - leaders of different political parties.

CHAPTER NINE

Who Is Not Guilty?

After a long time, he went to a friend's house. There he saw four rape-victims girls learning fencing.

He asked his friend "Why are you teaching them all this?"

"They themselves will tell you. Girls, what will be cut by the sharp edge of your sword?" The friend asked those girls.

"The look that turns evil upon us" said the first girl in a loud voice.

"The tongue that scoffs at us," said another girl excitedly.

"The hands that fall on our bodies." There was fire in the eyes of the third girl.

"And..?"

"And... that neck also, which keeps on bowing when an innocent is raped," the fourth girl cried.

Hearing this, his neck was cut with a sharp edge of shame.

CHAPTER TEN

Opportunistic Pieces of Chess

He had woken up as usual; but he saw that all the pieces of chess laid by him in the night were moving in unknown directions as soon as the morning light. All of them had also changed their speed. The knight was moving diagonally, the rook and the bishop were swapping places, the queen was crawling, the king had put on a pawn mask, and the pawns were scattered into different sections.

He shouted, "You all are my pieces, I have laid this chessboard, you have to move according to me." But all the pieces ignored his voice, and he could not even touch them when he extended his hand to wrap the chessboard.

He was surprised when the chessboard started flying in the air and went over his head. He looked up and on the back side of the chessboard was written - "Election's Results".

CHAPTER ELEVEN

Black Money won't be Eradicated

Two friends were talking amongst themselves.

One said, "Yesterday there was a revolution in the whole country. All the people holding black money from the government have been blamed."

The other asked in surprise, "How is that?"

The first replied, "Oh brother, you don't know! From yesterday, the big currency has been discontinued. This decision was given immediately. Now the old currency will be deposited only in the bank, and that too, up to a limit, cannot be used anywhere else. Tax will be imposed on depositing more than the limit. Those who have black money will not be able to get it deposited and then their black money will be trashed."

"Wow! This is a great and wise decision; we have gone a step ahead in eradicating black money." The other said happily.

"One step! Oh brother, a hundred percent black money will be eradicated." The first said, looking with confidence in the eyes of the other.

The other kept watching and listening to him silently.

The first asked again, "Okay! Tell me how much money you have kept in old currency?"

"I don't have much of anything," The other replied.

"Then you are the right person, I have some extra money with me, deposit it in your bank account and back it to me later after a few days."

The other smiled and nodded his head in a yes posture.

CHAPTER TWELVE

Untouchability

'A' went to the house of his friend 'B' for the first time. Seeing there, he said, "How wonderful your house is - clean and bright."

" The government has allotted. As compared to the untouchability suffered by ancestors, the job and residence provided by reservation is nothing. Let's drink tea.", 'B' replied.

The tea came, but 'B' stood up on seeing the one who brought it, and shouted from afar, "Keep the tea there... and go away...."

'A' asked, "What happened?"

"Hey! He's the one who cleans the toilet in the house and he is bringing the tea!"

CHAPTER THIRTEEN

Post Mortem of Relations

Dr. Steve had dedicated his whole life to considering his profession as service. He could provide little time for his family, but he also considered the fulfillment of all the wishes of the family members as his basic and necessary duty, which he did throughout his life. Today he was completing 54 years of his life. His family members had convinced him not to see any patients today. The birthday party was going on when the phone started ringing. A patient's condition was critical. Steve could not bear it and he went to the hospital before cutting the cake.

Dr. Steve returned around one o'clock in the night. He saw that the party was over and his wife and children were also asleep. The food items scattered in the room, empty drinks bottles, dancing floor etc. were telling that the party had completed happily, but the cake was kept as it is, uncut.

He went to the cake, and looking at it, said, "The birthday is over, even the wishers have fallen asleep and you are kept like a dead body. Let me do your post-mortem." and he picked up the knife kept nearby.

CHAPTER FOURTEEN

Meeting With the Creators

He took me along, he had to quietly search for a person.

At first, he met a well-known teacher, who was well-versed in talk, however, he passed his examinations by copying.

Then he visited a great doctor, who called his own method of medicine the best and the rest bad.

Then he met with three beggars, who used to beg in the name of their religion and used to hit their own family members every night. One of them was named beggar, the other the discourse and the third the leader.

Finally, they met with a corpse. She herself was silent, but her family members were crying loudly, although the money she left was in their minds.

He finally broke the silence, "It seems that I am creating humans out of words, not elements."

CHAPTER FIFTEEN

A Woman

"How beautiful do your eyes become after applying mascara?"
"Yes, my boss says the same thing."
"Well, your selection of clothes is also very good, perfect fit for you!"
"The boss feels the same"
"Oh, the makeup you put on your face, how much your color blossoms."
"Boss also says the exact same word ..."
"Oops .... I am your husband or boss?"
"Your eyes are not like a husband, these are like a boss, and otherwise there is a woman behind all this."

CHAPTER SIXTEEN

Blank News

One farmer was looking at the sky. The cloudless sky looked like a blank paper.

The headline in today's newspaper was that there has been a flood in Kashmir, the country's army is saving everyone. There was nothing bigger news than this in the whole country.

And without knowing this news, the farmer kept on looking at the sky.

CHAPTER SEVENTEEN

Treasure

In the evening after the father's funeral, the two sons were sitting in the courtyard outside the house with their relatives and neighbors. At this point, the wife of the elder son came and she said something to her husband's ear. The elder son gestured towards his younger brother to come in, looking at him with meaningful eyes and stood and folded his hands to the people sitting there and said, "Come in five minutes now".

Then both brothers went inside. As soon as they went inside, the elder brother whispered and said to the younger, "Look in the box, otherwise someone will come to assert it." The younger also nodded in agreement.

Going to the father's room, the elder brother's wife said to her husband, "Take out the box, I close the door." And she moved towards the door.

Both brothers bent under the bed and pulled out the box kept there. The elder brother's wife took out a key from her pocket and gave it to her husband.

As soon as the box opened, the three peeped into the box

with great curiosity. There were forty-fifty books kept inside. All three suddenly did not believe. The elder brother's wife said in a frustrated tone, "I was quite sure that when our father never took the money even for his medicine, then the money and jewels of his savings would be kept in this box, but nothing is in its..."

At that time the younger brother saw that in the corner of the box a cloth bag was placed near the books, he took out that bag. It had a few rupees and a paper with it. Curiosity struck the faces of all three as soon as they saw the money. The younger brother counted the money and then read the paper, it was written in that,

"My funeral's expenses"

CHAPTER EIGHTEEN

The pen woke up

Waking up to the writer sleeping in the garden, an old man asked, "Why are you sleeping here?"

"Was writing a speech on independence for a minister, I got tired of thinking and fell asleep." The author replied, while waking up.

"What will you get in return?", the old man asked again.

"I will get money.", the author replied.

"If your pen was not subject to money and would wake up the sleeping people and tell them that they are also free, then you too would not get tired of thinking."

On hearing that, the writer felt the open air of the garden for the first time.

CHAPTER NINETEEN

Is God too Indulged in Corruption?

A man went to a minister, gave him some money and said, "Allow me to increase the love of the countrymen for God."

The minister gave permission.

He first started selling counterfeit medicines and later got many temples built.

CHAPTER TWENTY

Midnight Sun

“You know, son, the sun shines even at midnight in Norway.”

"Then, daddy, means, no thefts would happen there?" The son asked guessing.

“It happens, when people sleep there with curtains on, the sunlight shows the way to thieves...”

At that time, he suddenly remembered the soldiers of the night patrol.

CHAPTER TWENTY-ONE

The Holy Sinner

"Do you know, now that prostitute has had a bad relationship with Ramesh too," The wife of the priest told Savitri, who had come to worship.

"Yeah, I know." Savitri replied.

"Take care of your husband. Ramesh lives very near to your house."

"It is probably not even in God's hands to take care of it", at that time Savitri looked at the priest and his face bowed. Savitri's broken bangle was still crying in the deserted area outside the temple.

CHAPTER TWENTY-TWO

Who is not a thief?

"My servant went away after stealing my money." He said to his friend.

The friend said, "He who builds his house with dishonesty and stealing money can never be happy."

The victim looked at the friend in shock and said distraughtly, "No, it doesn't happen these days."

And he could not say, "Even my house was also built with this only..."

CHAPTER TWENTY-THREE

Opened Doors for Abuses

Seeing her son's questioning eyes outside the labor room, his mother made a bad face and said, " burnt-karma-holder, black-faced, your wife has given birth to a daughter again."

Listening this, her son's eldest daughter asked, "grandmother, who gives birth to a daughter, is a burnt-karma-holder and black-faced?"

"Yeah, and wretched too..."

"Then Grandma, your mother also..."

CHAPTER TWENTY-FOUR

Poisonous Person

"While catching the poisonous snakes, now your brain has also got poisoned, Hari, the snake charmer. If your wife is missing for two days, then search for her somewhere else. She is not here."

"Zamindar sir, the people of the village have seen that your son took her to your mansion..."

"It's all a lie." Zamindar shouted out, "Listen... is somebody here... tell him to go out..."

And snake charmer Hari shockingly understood that not all poisonous dance on his instructions.

CHAPTER TWENTY-FIVE

Need for Fees

"Where are you going?"

"To the Guru, to be freed from bondage"

"Then this money?"

"For the fee of Guru, how can one get salvation without offering this?"

CHAPTER TWENTY-SIX

Permanent Picture

"I always see photographs of terrorists in your shop. Why do you put so?"

"I am a butcher by caste, sir. I've slaughtered many animals, but till today, I couldn't cut those animals, whose photographs I put, nor any soldier. I hope, one day I will put a picture of that person who will cut these animals."

CHAPTER TWENTY-SEVEN

Never Faith Blindly

"He took advantage of the darkness, and rapped me..." said Rajni, crying.

"But why did you go with him in the dark?" the Judge asked.

"Blind faith was there... the eyes of the mind covered up the eyes of the body... honourable Judge..."

CHAPTER TWENTY-EIGHT

Won't take brains from these skulls

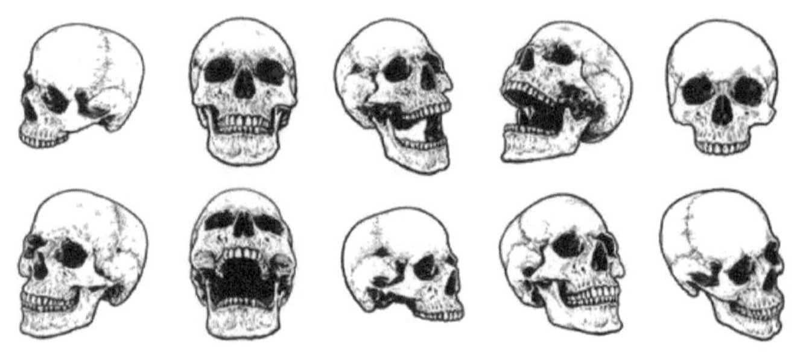

In the palm-gadget glowing in the open palm of his left hand, the person opted for 'quick writing with marks' and then 'excursion review' with the right finger. The date and place automatically began to appear at the top of the gadget:

15 December 2121

Location: Ancient Museum, India.

Now he pressed down with the finger of his right hand some of the buttons protruding on the gadget. Following words were being appeared automatically on the screen at the top of the gadget.

I went to the Antique Museum with my family for 45 minutes. In these 45 minutes we had to see and understand only 5 objects of the museum. But I couldn't see five things. Looking at the second item, my son Ehtisham took me to that table. On that six hundred year old skulls were put together. He asked, "What is the difference between all these skulls?" I looked carefully but didn't understand anything.

I called my wife Bronie and asked her from a gesture, she also looked at those skulls for a while and shook her head in a posture of no. Now I looked around and saw that there was an inquiry tool nearby. I was glad that I have been able to answer my son's curiosity. The three of us sat down on the auto-detection chairs and set the listening distance and frequency by placing our thumbs on the small EarSound screen in the device. In the next two seconds, there was a stir in the big screen in front of our eyes and the people of a hundred years old civilization came to the fore.

And there was a surprise! The video was surprising. All skulls were belonged to humans. But one of them identified as a Christian, the other a Muslim, the third a Hindu and the fourth a Sikh. The fifth skull was of a low caste and the sixth skull was that of a eunuch. At that time, they were all considered different.

Words kept coming out of my mouth. Without wasting time, at first I unset ear frequency of Ehtisham's and later on both of us. Then I turned off the display screen. I gestured to Bronie not to bring our daughter, Kirat, who is learning how to grow old trees with robots in today's environment.

Before broadcasting this review to all of you, I've also sent the museum manager a quick video of the futuristic effect of this display made by my personal Auto Thought Understanding Robo, in which it's clear that these skulls and their interrogation tools should be removed from the museum immediately. Otherwise it will create destructive pollution in the mind of our children.

broadcast human

- Vocal

While writing this he closed the palm of his left hand and, pressing his little finger of the same hand twice, closed the palm-gadget, then took out a tablet of the smile-supplementer from the drawer of the table and placed it in his mouth.

CHAPTER TWENTY-NINE

The Divinity of Black Money

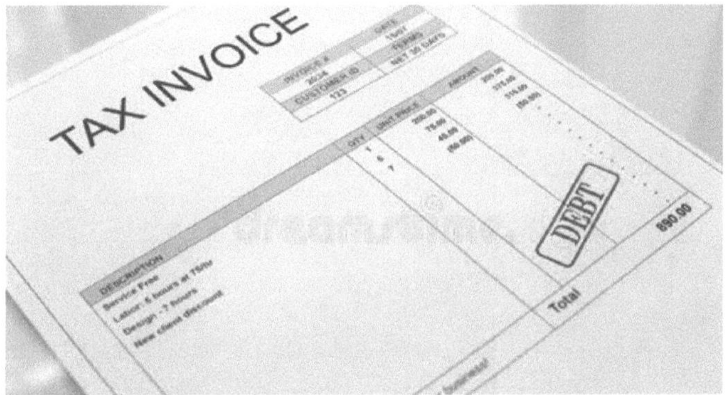

While buying a painkiller pill at the drugstore, Robert was proudly saying, “Heard James, what a wonderful way our country’s President adopted is getting the black money out. He is the Messiah, he said, that all these black money people should be put in jail, and all the money should be distributed among the poor."

“Perfectly, they have also given a call that whatever you buy, definitely take the bill; otherwise these shopkeepers earn black money." James replied.

"Yeah, right, so brother, give the bill to us too." Robert spoke to the shopkeeper with a very serious attitude.

The shopkeeper said the very next moment, "Of course sir, but you will have to pay the tax separately."

"Oh no! Then let it be, I don't have any extra money." Saying that both the hands of Robert were in his pocket of the paint.

CHAPTER THIRTY

Earnings of Life-long

Two friends separated at a young age, met at an old age in a playground. While hugging, both of them slipped from the stairs.

While sitting there, one asked, "How much money have you earned?"

"Not much, only that much, which is necessary for living."

"It means you live life honestly. To earn, it is also necessary to lay the foundation of dishonesty somewhere." said the first friend with a laugh.

Both stood up but both experienced lameness because of the fall. Seeing which, the secretary of the first friend handed him a gold stick and the son of the other gave him shoulder support.

About The Author

Enter Caption

Dr. Chandresh Kumar Chhatlani has over 20 years of rich experience in Training, Research, Academics, Writing, Software Development, Website Development and Design Developed more than 140 software & websites independently). Dr. Chhatlani has adequate experience of all types of documentation and dealing with NAAC Assessment, UGC, AICTE, MHRD, NIRF, Distance Education, AISHE, Supreme Court, PCI, CCH etc. along with organizing conferences, seminars and workshops. He has earned more than 1000 certificates from Microsoft, Amity, Cisco, Google, IEEE, Diksha, WHO and other reputed institutes. Dr. Chandresh has received 10 national/ international awards. Chandresh is writing Stories, Short Stories and Poems. More than 100 Stories / Short Stories and 30 poems published in various Books, Magazines, Newspapers, Websites and Blogs of National and International repute.

9 798886 410204

Printed by Libri Plureos GmbH in Hamburg,
Germany